What Shall I Fear?

Cathy Brown Hathaway

Cathy Brown Hathaway
(423) 987-7321
Cathat44@gmail.com
www.cathat44.wix.com

4-P Publishing

Chattanooga, TN 37411

ISBN # 978-1-941749-29-6

~ v ~

Dedication

This book is dedicated to my friend,

my husband, Gary.

Acknowledgements

Thank you to

Coach Laura Brown for your vision. Without you this book would not exist.

Wayne Brown for planting the seed.

My son, Anthony, for protecting his Mom.

Rosalyn Brown for the best advice I've received since becoming a minister's and pastor's wife: "Just be yourself." A simple, yet profound statement.

Wenda Johnson for being my cheerleader. You reflect God's love.

Sonia Toliver for your encouragement and allowing me to vent.

My support team: Gloria McKeldin, Suzanne James, Barbaree Simmons, Mary Green, Doris Tibbs, Rita Lockhart, Tonya O'Guinn.

About the Author

Cathy Brown Hathaway is a retired Postmaster. She is active in church and community service organizations as a teacher, speaker and musician. She is founder of Jewels of God (JOG) Ministry which provides mentoring for young adult women. She is also founder of the Lovely Bones Book Club in Chattanooga, TN.

What Shall I Fear is her first novel. She resides in Chattanooga, TN with her husband, Gary. They have one son, Anthony.

Available for seminars, workshops and motivational speaking. Call (423) 987-7321.

Contents

Introduction..1

Chapter 1...3

Chapter 2...11

Chapter 3...15

Chapter 4...21

Chapter 5...29

Chapter 6...37

Chapter 7...43

Chapter 8...51

Chapter 9...55

Chapter 10..63

Chapter 11..77

Chapter 12..91

Chapter 13..97

Chapter 14...105

Chapter 15...115

Chapter 16 119

References 125

Introduction

Fear is an emotion we have trouble keeping at bay. It creeps in unexpectedly and clouds our decisions, our actions and our behavior. Oftentimes, we don't identify it until we've become overwhelmed. Joyce Meyer says it best in 'The Everyday Life Bible':

I am going to tell you a little secret: fear will never stop coming against us. We must learn to do what God tells us to do whether we feel fear or not. We must "do it afraid" if necessary, but that is what courage does; it feels the fear and does what it should anyway!

I always thought that as long as I felt fear, I was a coward, but I have learned differently. When God told Joshua repeatedly to fear not (see Joshua 1:9; 10:8), He let him know that fear was going to attack him, but that he must walk in obedience to what God spoke.

We are not cowards because we feel fear. We are cowards only if we let fear rule our decisions.

Paula Kennedy is about to discover how fear is clouding her world. Will she allow her faith to triumph over fear?

Chapter 1

As I hold the phone to my ear waiting for the tele-conference to begin, I replay the conversation with Uncle Ron in my head.

"I know you're a career woman with major responsibilities, but you are the one person I can count on to keep Linn in check. It has been three days since she injured her knee and Dr. Morris gave specific instructions for her to stay off her feet for at least a week. I cannot keep her still."

"You can count on me Uncle Ron. Give me a couple of days to clear my calendar and make sure Jason is okay."

Uncle Ron breathed a sigh of relief and said, "I'll be at the conference through Friday morning. I'll have a quick lunch and should be home before 6:00pm."

"Anything for my favorite Uncle."

The voice of the facilitator comes on the phone and for the next forty-five minutes, I am engrossed in customer service, budget and safety issues. I treasure this job. No two days are the same and every (EVERY) day is a challenge.

--

The call from Uncle Ron is really a blessing in disguise. He is off to a pastor's conference and I'm spending the next few days with Aunt Linn. I'm hoping she can help me sort through some concerns I have about my role as a pastor's wife. She seems to embrace the role. But, Aunt Linn embraces life. She is quite versatile and very much the social butterfly.

Of course, my role will be to 'support' my husband. As a wife I will 'support' my husband. But, what does it really mean as a pastor's wife? A pastor's wife has a unique position with unique concerns. I think Aunt Linn maybe that blessing in disguise.

--

On the way home from work, Pappadeaux's Restaurant provides me with Jason's favorite dinner. I'm hoping he will be receptive to me going away for a few days to help Aunt Linn. With dinner, my attaché case and a shoulder purse in tow, I exit the elevator on the 3rd floor, our home. We purchased this small, 3-story office building in Knoxville, TN at a steal and use the top floor as our residence. We left the space open with no walls separating the rooms. The elevator opens to the kitchen where Jason sits at the counter.

Jason and I met as freshmen at Howard University. He was an engineering major and I was in journalism/public relations. He was standing behind me in line at the bookstore and noticed we were purchasing the same book. We began talking and there was an instant attraction. I was admiring his chiseled body and handsome face as he talked. I suppose he liked what he saw too. He said, "You are gorgeous. Your eyes are intoxicating." "Good line," I thought. We dated off and on, and in our senior year decided to think about the future. We began to talk about marriage.

Jason would write these corny poems on my birthday and Valentine's Day. It was our senior year in college, Valentine's Day. We had a picnic lunch in the park and were sitting in a swing. Pushing us back and forth he said,

"Paula, Paula hair so fair
A question for you, shall I dare
I think you love me, if this be true
Marry me, Paula? Never again will I be blue."

I began laughing and made no comment. He stopped the swing and said, "I'm serious. I want us to be together after we graduate." I stopped laughing and stared at him. My hands went to my mouth. Tears rolled down my cheeks as I said, "I want that too." One year after college graduation, we were married.

Jason is sitting at the counter going through the mail when I enter the kitchen. He's still wearing his work clothes, without the gray suit jacket. His gold tie hangs loosely around his neck, continuing to accent his crisp white shirt. The shirt looks as neat as it did when he left for work this morning. Sometimes I wonder if he ever sweats.

"Hey Babe," I said.

Looking up he said, "Hi!   Something smells good!"

"Your favorite," I said.

"Let me help you with those bags," he said laughing.

"How was your day?" I asked.

"It was good. Busy, but good."

"Uncle Ron called today."

"Really?"

"Yes." I explained Aunt Linn's injury and Uncle Ron's request.

"Can you get away from work?"

"I think so. I'll make sure everything is covered. My back-up will be on hand for emergencies. Work should be fine. Will you?"

"I'm never fine when you're away," he said.

I walk over and embrace him.   "I love you," I said.

"I love you too."

Chapter 2

The next day at work, I began to clear my calendar for my trip to Brownville, Georgia. Five minutes later my first appointment arrives early. After putting on my hunter green suit jacket, I gather my paperwork. While straightening the matching skirt, I check the light green and yellow blouse in the small mirror next to my desk. I retrieve his file and meet him in the conference room.

After checking his application, I find Mr. Harrison does not have all the necessary documents to complete the interview process. A telephone call prior to the interview made it clear what was needed to complete the hiring process. Again, I explain the timeline to Mr. Harrison. He has pending issues in another state which prevent him from finalizing this process. He assures me that it will be resolved soon and all paperwork will be in place. After Mr. Harrison leaves, I gather the papers and stuff them into his file. I shake my head and wonder if I want this job for him more than he does.

Returning to my desk, I place the file in the pending stack. Pulling my calendar out again, I answer my ringing phone, "Human Resources, Paula Kennedy."

Chapter 3

The next day, as I leave for Brownville, Jason is leaving for work. I'm looking forward to some 'downtime'. My last day at work was monstrous. Tying up loose ends coupled with all day interviews left me drained. A few days to relax will be good.

With my snacks for the road, new jazz cd's and a need to recharge, I set out for Brownville. Listening to Kirk Whalum's *The Gospel According to Jazz* begins to calm my spirit. I've been anxious and uneasy lately. It's not work. Work is good; very busy, but that's the norm. It's not Jason. Our relationship is good; we work at it. Is it me? The answer doesn't come quickly.

Is it the role of First Lady? My usual level head is challenged. Not one to run from a challenge, I'm puzzled at my hesitancy. What's blocking the tenacious drive I normally exhibit? Maybe Aunt Linn has found that Pastors' Wives Handbook she jokes about. When dealing with issues at church she would say, "I still haven't found the Pastors' Wives Handbook. The bookstores don't have it. I can't find it on the internet. I'll go where I should have begun – the Bible."

It has taken many sessions of banging my head against the wall for that lesson to sink in.
There will be no head banging this week.

--

When my scenic drive home to Brownville was taken away by the expressway many years ago, I was disappointed. I enjoyed driving through small towns and taking mental snapshots of country living – relishing the slower pace and relishing the quiet.

I'm fifteen miles from Brownville and notice the large fields of peanuts and cotton spreading for miles. There are massive irrigation systems looming over the fields ready to quench their thirst.

Each visit home brings memories of Uncle Weston's farm. There were miles of various types of vegetables, farm animals, and land. As children, we were under foot; in Uncle Weston's way.

Crossing the bridge that signals "home", I see the lovely waterfall to my right. On the left is the Highway 37 Diner which has been closed since I was in middle school.

I relax. I'm home, Brownville, Georgia.

--

When I arrive at Uncle Ron's home he's packing his SUV to leave for his pastor's conference. He straightens his 6' 2" frame and walks toward me. Wearing tan slacks, a tan silk sweater and brown loafers, he's ready for travel. He grins and gives me a bear hug and a "thank you". We chat briefly, then he dashes in the house a final time. He comes back out, takes the steps two at a time and hops into the SUV. He waves goodbye and he's gone.

As I enter the beautiful ranch style home where my Uncle grew up, I admire its' lovely antique furnishings that are a testament to his wife's good taste. Aunt Linn is resting in an overstuffed lounger.

"Hi, Aunt Linn."

"Hello, Paula. I'm so glad you were able to come. I told Ron I would be fine while he is away, but he insisted that someone be with me. I'm happy it's you that he called."

"It's always good to visit you and Uncle Ron. This is actually an opportune time for me.
I needed some time away. "

"Excellent! I hope you won't mind taking me to my doctors' appointments and meetings I have scheduled this week."

"Of course, Aunt Linn. That's the reason I'm here."

Chapter 4

The following day, I wake up at 5:30 for my morning run. I stumble to the bathroom to wash my face. In the mirror I see the reflection of my grandfather who was a Cherokee Indian. I have his eyes, a cross between light green and brown. I also have his fair skin tone. Returning home always brings a rush of memories of my grandparents.

After washing my face and brushing my teeth, I dress in black biker shorts and a black tee shirt. Having also inherited my grandfather's brown curly hair, I tie my shoulder length tresses in a ponytail and add a red ribbon.

Grabbing a water bottle from the refrigerator, I'm out the door.

--

An hour later, sweaty and exhilarated, I'm searching the refrigerator for an energy drink. Armed with my cold drink, I look for Aunt Linn.

Aunt Linn tore her ACL while playing the final game of a state championship tennis match. Being an avid tennis player, she refused to forfeit the game. She and her partner won the match and first place in their division. She also won time out from tennis until her knee heals. One of her perks as comptroller for Windermere Resorts is being able to work from home.   She said the injured knee has not affected her work, and she's actually accomplishing more at home, having less distractions.

My Aunt and Uncle lead an active life style. During a visit shortly after they married, I went to the garage for a can of paint. I was amazed at the grown-up toys: canoes, golf clubs, bicycles, motorcycles...

When Uncle Ron talks about her a smile creeps across his face. He told me when he decided to settle down he asked God to send him a companion. Shortly afterwards, he met Aunt Linn.

This morning I find Aunt Linn on the flower lined deck. Luscious, tall palms sit in each corner of the deck. She's sitting in a yellow cushioned wicker chair and nursing a steaming cup of coffee.

"Good morning, Aunt Linn."

"Good morning. I didn't expect you up this early."

"I thought I would get a jog in before the heat kicks in."

"Great idea, Paula. Wish I could join you."

"I wish you could too. You might help me sort through a few things as we jog."

"What's bothering you, Paula?

"I don't know how to be a pastor's wife."

"Who does?" questioned Aunt Linn.

"Paula, the best advice given to me since my husband became a minister and pastor is to 'be yourself'. There is no instruction book on "How to be a Pastor's Wife", but there are women in those shoes who would gladly share their joys and challenges with you."

--

After breakfast, I drive a few miles from town, and make a turn on the road to Uncle Weston's farm. Replacing the empty lot on the corner is a lovely southern style home. The house is surrounded by a white fence. The lush lawn has strategically placed flower beds. A gazebo sits to one side awaiting a reader with an open book. The bridge perched over a sparkling stream invites a leisurely walk. The one level house has a welcoming façade with white rocking chairs gracing the front porch.

I later learn the house is owned by Uncle Weston's former neighbor who moved to Philadelphia years ago. He returned home after retirement and chose this site for his new home.

Driving slowly, I approach the 4-way stop. The big gray, haunted house which sat back to the right is gone. As children we would play in the yard there and my Uncle would scare us senseless. He would run from the back yard, out of breath and say, "I saw a man with no head. He's behind the house." Of course, we believed him. Everyone would scream and run.

Approaching Uncle Weston's house, I noted 'spots' on each side of the road where we would park the car and pick luscious blackberries. Driving a few more yards, I see the 'spots' where we picked juicy red plums.

I make the left turn into Uncle Weston's drive. Uncle Weston was tall and masculine with a commanding presence. His skin was tanned from working in the sun. His practical clothes indicated he was always working. He had a booming laugh that made children giggle.

After parking the Audi, I gaze at the vacant white house that smelled of cakes and cooking preserves. For a child, this farm was like the Land of Oz, miles and miles of excitement. Riding on the back of Uncle Weston's truck at his farm was magical. On the right, cows grazed in the field. On the left was an endless field of corn. Behind the house was a huge barn next to the pig pen. There was a hen house nestled into a plot bordering the corn field. A dirt road led to a cucumber patch, watermelons, cotton, squash . . . Returning to this place of my childhood is always calming. The stillness and memories are balm for my soul.

Chapter 5

I decide to sleep late this morning so it's warm when I began to jog. Dressed in matching red biker shorts and t-shirt, I jog pass Ms. Edith's house with the 'Beware of Dog' sign in the front yard; the same sign that I ignored in high school and resulted in a dog bite on my right leg, a tetanus shot, and a permanent scar. Planning to ride to school with my classmate, Jerry, I sashayed into his yard, reading the large 'Beware of Dog' sign. I thought nothing of it and walked to the front door. Simultaneously, I heard a loud growl and felt his dog's teeth clamp around my ankle. Everything was a blur after that. My parents took me to the doctor and refused the offer from Jerry's parents to cover medical expenses. There was no major damage; only permanent bite marks. Needless to say, I didn't ride to school with Jerry again.

Further down the street, a charming new house sits in the lot across from Mr. Mosely's home. He and my grandfather were good friends. When I was a child visiting my grandparents on Friday evenings, I would hear a horn blow. Peeking through the curtains, I would see Mr. Mosely parked in front of the house, waiting for Grandpa. Closing the curtains, I would turn to see Grandpa cleaned-up and smelling good. They were headed for some fun.

According to rumor, Mr. Mosely's son purchased the lot and built the house for his father. Mr. Mosely prefers to live in the house where his children were born so the new house remains vacant.

I approach the Recreation Center, the teenage hangout during high school. If walls could talk... I saw the good, the bad, and the ugly here. I remember an incident when we were teenagers hanging out on the weekend. We were idling around the grounds, sitting on car hoods, passing the time. I was hanging with my neighbor, Jerry. My girlfriend's car was parked next to Jerry's car. I hopped on the hood of her car and allowed my legs to dangle over the side near Jerry's car. Not paying attention, Jerry got in his car and while backing up turned the wheel and plunged his car into the same ankle his dog bit. I screamed in pain.

He immediately recognized his mistake and released my crushed ankle. After apologizing profusely, he took me home. A trip to the doctor cleared me of any major damage. I never again sat on the hood of a car.

I reach my Cousin Shelley's house. Shelley was the drop-off point when my father would send my sister on a date with me. We dropped my sister off at Shelley's house.

Breathing hard, I decide to reverse my direction. My legs are getting weak. I think I'll walk back.

--

Aunt Linn has finished eating breakfast when I enter the kitchen.

"I'm sorry Aunt Linn. I was late getting up this morning. I shortened my run so you wouldn't have to wait too long for breakfast."

"It's okay Paula. I'm injured, not helpless. I fixed some cinnamon-raisin toast and coffee. There's some for you on the counter."

"You didn't have to do that! I'm here to take care of you."

"Sit down and eat," she said.

"Yes, Sergeant," I said. Aunt Linn laughed.

"I want to ask you something that concerns me."

"Do you feel that you can really be yourself as a pastor's wife?"

"Sure," she said. "As a matter-of-fact, I've learned how to keep my mouth shut. Some things are better left unsaid. You may think you have to always take the high road, but that's not only for the pastor's wife - - that's for all Christians."

"You're right," I say as I finish breakfast.

"Are you ready for your doctor's appointment?"

"I am," she said.

Chapter 6

In the doctor's waiting room, a rambunctious 2 year old boy is playing with his older brother who appears to be around six. His older brother is trying to ignore him, but he's not having it. Their mother is oblivious to the banter going on between them. She's enjoying last month's issue of Ebony magazine.

Aunt Linn has been with the doctor for an hour when the nurse calls me into the doctor's office. The doctor is an attractive African American woman with an easy smile. As she stands to shake my hand, I notice her beautiful pale yellow, tailored suit. She wears no make-up and her skin is flawless. Her features remind me of the actress, Debbie Allen.

"Don't get alarmed", says Aunt Linn. "Everything is fine. I wanted you to meet Dr. Juanita Pace. She's not only my doctor, but my friend and a pastor's wife."

"It's good to meet you Dr. Pace."

"And you as well, Paula. I have a few minutes before my next patient. Linn tells me you have some concerns about your role as a pastor's wife."

"I do, Dr. Pace. If you don't mind me asking, what is it that you enjoy most as a pastor's wife?"

"Well," answered Dr. Pace. "That's not the question I expected. I suppose the best thing for me is watching my husband do what he loves to do, which is teaching and preaching – knowing that he is sincere."

"I've heard some interesting answers to that question. One pastor's wife told me the thing she enjoys most is living with a Biblical scholar. Having someone you can ask biblical questions 24/7 is a blessing to her."

As Dr. Pace answers her phone, I stand to leave. "I know you're busy," I said. "Thank you for talking to me."

"My pleasure. When you're in town, stop by and say hello."

"I will."

Chapter 7

Aunt Linn is resting after her doctor's appointment.

I enjoy some jazz music as I put the finishing touches on dinner. Uncle Ron has a massive collection of jazz cd's. When I was in high school, we would play 'guess the artist'. He would be amazed that I knew the names of jazz musicians. Uncle Ron still has the trumpet he played in the high school band. He plays it during those moments of deja vu.

After switching off the music, I look for Aunt Linn. I find her in the study surrounded by walls of books.

"Have you read all these books Aunt Linn?"

"Most of them," she answered. "Ron has put a few on the shelves. Most of his are in his office."

"I suppose reading keeps you sharp," I said.

"It's entertainment, Paula. Reading a good book is like watching a good movie."

"If you can tear yourself away from your entertainment, dinner is ready."

"It smells delicious," said Aunt Linn.

"I tried a new recipe for the meat sauce. It might be a bit spicy."

"I'm sure it's fine."

"Paula, when you were talking to Dr. Pace today, I thought back to the day Ron told me he had been called into the ministry. Like you, I also wondered what that meant for me. After beating myself over the head with that question until it hurt, I finally asked God for guidance. I could have saved myself a headache if I had gone to God first. What that meant for me was to continue doing what God had already shown me to do."

"I un-der-stand Aunt Linn. That's good!"

"When Jason became a minister I had this feeling, Aunt Linn. There was this feeling that

I needed to be perfect. Jason didn't make me feel this way. This was self-imposed. Over the years, I learned that I had higher expectations of myself than anyone else. A friend reminded me of a scripture in the Bible (2 Corinthians 3:17) that says where the Spirit of the Lord is, there is liberty. That is so true. I am free to be myself. I don't have to second guess my decisions; what I say or what I do. I'm free."

"Enough about me. How's the spaghetti sauce?"

"Excellent."

--

After dinner I browse the study for something to read. I notice a picture of Uncle Ron and my mother as children. In the picture they are playing kickball in the yard. Tears roll down my cheeks as I remember the worst day of my life.

It was my junior year in college. A call came from my father while I was studying for final exams. My mother had died unexpectedly of a heart attack. She was 42 years old. My world was shattered. I don't know how I managed the next few months, but that's when I recognized my bond with Jason. Jason's spiritual strength at such a young age amazed me. He held my hand, wiped my tears and shared the love of God with me. Already being in love with him, that may have sealed the deal. One day Jason left a letter in my book bag that still consoles me when I'm missing my mother:

Paula,

I know you're feeling the loss of your mother, but please know that I feel it too. Because I love you, I feel your pain. Please don't think you're alone. I'm here.

If you need to cry, you have my shoulder. If you need a hug, you have my embrace. If you need to talk, call me.

God is here too, Paula. You can talk to him just as you talk to me. What I can't do, God can.

I Love You.

Jason

Wiping my eyes, I return the picture to the bookshelf.

There's a mound of magazines on a table with more family photos. I choose House and Garden and head to my room.

--

My eyes open and the bedside light is still on. The House and Garden magazine has slipped off the bed to the floor. I dreamed of my mother -- cannot recount details. A warm feeling envelops me. My mother is telling me, "You're fine Paula. You're right where you should be. God has not given you the spirit of fear. He loves you and will see you through any challenge."

I switch the light off and fall back asleep.

Chapter 8

It's 9:30am when I park my Audi A6 in the parking lot of Roses Department Store. This is the first long distance trip I've taken in my new car. Jason surprised me with it on my birthday. My Honda Accord was on its' last leg. I look in the rearview mirror, turn and look over my shoulder, and have that odd feeling I had yesterday morning. Walking back from my morning run, I had the feeling that someone was watching me. I'm sure it's nothing.

Inside the store, with Aunt Linn's shopping list in hand, I began scanning the aisles. I see a familiar face from high school and as I approach her to say hello, I see the face of the person she's talking to and stop dead in my tracks.

My mind travels back to the last year of high school when my first love dropped me for a younger, cuter version. I was smarter - - that didn't matter. He broke my heart. I haven't seen him since graduation and there he stands, looking the same: 5' 9" tall, honey brown complexion, close haircut and hooded eyes that see through you. Dressed in his signature black slacks and black t-shirt, he still looks good. I'm paralyzed. Mind in a fog. Legs won't move. After a few seconds, I turn around, leave the buggy with Aunt Linn's booty and exit the store. I get in the Audi and drive to another store.

Chapter 9

I park on the 'square' downtown. It's actually a circular street around the courthouse. As I look for another store to purchase Aunt Linn's items, I spot a vintage hat in the window of an antique store. I walk in the store, check the price and quickly replace it on the rack. After browsing through the store, I leave with a smile and a bag full of treasures.

Walking out of the antique shop I almost collide with a tall, fair skin, handsome man.

"I'm sorry," he said.

"No. I'm sorry. I wasn't watching where," I stop mid-sentence. "Mr.   Conner!"   I   say   with excitement.

"Paula Brown," he said.

"It's Paula Kennedy now. It's good to see you."

"Good to see you, as well," he said. "You're still beautiful."

"Thank you. Are you still teaching Chemistry?"

"I am", he said. "I'm also coaching basketball this year. If you're home during the season, come by and support us."

"I'll look forward to it."

Mr. Conner was a great teacher. He loved his students and they loved him. His wife was my girl scout leader and mentor.

"How is Mrs. Conner?"

"She's good. I'll tell her you're in town." He hurries away while I search my purse for Aunt Linn's shopping list.

--

After shopping, I drive through the neighborhood where my grandparents lived. The wooded area next to their property where we played Tarzan and Jane has been replaced by houses. The space for Grandmama's garden is now a 2-car garage. Her house remains in tact with additional rooms and trendy landscaping.

Further down the street, the community store/café/club is now a service station-convenience store. During my preteen years, while visiting my grandmother, I would sneak to the café to spend my money. You could buy candy and soda, and dance. It was quite tame by today's standards. But, my grandmother's preference was not to go alone. As a pre-teen, I was fearless – I went alone.

Turning onto the next street, I see the home of my friend, Patricia Brownley. It remains the same. She and I would rush home from school to watch soap operas. Then we would call each other and discuss the episodes. Pat's mother introduced the art of soap making to me. Pat and I would play in the backyard while her mother was stirring a concoction in a huge black iron pot. It was pot-ash. It was soap.

I turn into Pat's driveway, hoping someone is at home. There are no cars and the house looks quiet. Walking to the door, I remember the last time I saw Pat was at graduation. After ringing the doorbell twice with no answer, I conclude my walk down memory lane and return to the Audi.

--

I arrive at Aunt Linn's sorority meeting just as she exits the building. She's excited about an upcoming project the group is working on. They partner with high schools and mentor teenage girls. Having no children of her own, Aunt Linn gravitates towards children. When we go out, children – young and old – approach her with a smile and a hug. In college, she developed programs for her sorority that benefited disenfranchised youth.

"How was your meeting?" I asked.

"It was good. We're trying hard to impact the lives of teenage girls, but there are so many negative forces tugging at them. We're working with 10th – 12th graders, trying to meet them where they are and guide them to where they want to be. Some of them have not thought about tomorrow. They are too busy trying to make it through today. Oftentimes, we judge them too harshly. We don't know their background or their home environment. We have no idea what some of these young girls deal with each day."

"We would like to get them involved in planning and implementing programs," she said.
"Hopefully, this will identify their strengths and help develop some useful skills."

"You seem to be passionate about this Aunt Linn."

"I suppose I am. God blesses us and we have to pass it on."

Chapter 10

Back at Aunt Linn's, I find a red velvet cake in the refrigerator. A slice of cake and a cup of coffee might help Aunt Linn feel better. I put 2 cups of coffee and 2 slices of cake on a tray and join her in the den.

"How is your ankle?" I asked.

"It's had better days."

"Too much activity today?"

"I may have over done it. That's my typical scenario - - feeling good, keep moving, can't move. Common sense isn't in the equation."

"The doctor has ordered coffee and cake. Consume all of it and feel better in fifteen minutes." Aunt Linn laughed and devoured her cake.

"I saw Lewis in Roses this morning. I reacted like a silly teenager. I couldn't speak to him."

"Really!" she said. "What were you afraid of?"

"I – don't—know. I guess I was afraid of feeling rejection again."

"I don't want to preach to you, Paula. But, the Bible speaks of Jesus being rejected. That didn't stop him. Fear can be paralyzing. It can stagnate your life. We need to ask God to keep those emotions from becoming overwhelming. And, he will do it."

"Okay", she said. "This ends my sermon for today." We laughed.

"You're right," I said. "Fear has been creeping in a lot lately. I need to remember to 'suit-up' spiritually. I get busy and don't take the time to commune with God daily. Starting my day with meditation and prayer makes it so much easier. I can go through the day in peace. What a commodity. There's nothing like the peace of God."

"Alright," I said. "Now that we've had church, let's take up the offering." We laughed again.

"I have another question about your role as a pastor's wife."

"Sure."

"I'm afraid of being overwhelmed because I don't know how to say no. Did you have that problem?"

"I did in the beginning. There's a lot of work in Christian ministry. Your husband has a vision and you want to help see it come to fruition. But, you have to involve others. God has given us all talents and gifts. Allow them to be used. Don't let them lay dormant. You may have to coax and encourage to get people involved, but they will be glad you did. And so will you."

"Today," she said, "I can say no. It's a learning process. Your husband has found his calling. You have to find your calling. Where does your talent lie?"

"That's something I need to think about."

"I'm going to call Jason before I turn in," I said. "See you in the morning."

--

This morning I step outside for my morning run and hear the birds chirping. The smell of roses tickles my nostrils. I jog toward the school and stop at Shelley's house. Again, I walk back. When I pass the school, the sensation of someone watching me returns. I scan the parking lot and see no one. Across the street, no one is outside. Again, I dismiss it. Too much television.

--

I arrive at Mrs. Conner's home at 2:00pm. She is coordinating the mentoring program for Aunt Linn's sorority. In elementary school, Mrs. Conner was my role model. I was fascinated by her interest in me and my friends. A pretty, young teacher; she would take us to college football games and have us over for sleep-overs. Always smiling, she was the big sister who 'had our backs'. Today, she's still pretty, wearing a pink sleeveless jumpsuit. Her green sandals expose pink toenails.

Mrs. Conner greets me with an embrace. "It's so good to see you Paula."

"It's good to see you too."

"Linn talks about you often. She's so proud of you. Come in and visit with me. You look wonderful."

"Thank you."

"Is Linn following doctor's orders?" she asks.

"I think you know the answer to that one," I laughed. "I ran into Mr. Conner downtown. He looks great. Looks like you're taking good care of him."

"He's doing well," she said smiling. "Coaching basketball seems to put a little pep in his step."

"Linn told me Jason has been called to pastor a local church. Are you excited about it?"

"I am excited, but also a bit unsure of my role as his wife."

"My mother is a pastor's wife," Mrs. Conner said. "I didn't understand her unique position until I became an adult. She told me one of her biggest challenges was wearing too many hats. One day she realized she needed to share some of those hats. She understood she didn't have to be involved in every program of the church."

"It sounds like she spread herself too thin," I said.

"You're right. She had no time to relax and enjoy leisurely time with her husband. Sometimes we get so caught up we forget the important things. Today she's focusing on the Youth Department – her passion."

"I'll keep that in mind," I said.

"Tell Linn to remember our meeting with the girls next week."

--

Reaching for my cellphone to call Aunt Linn at the tennis center, I realize it's on the kitchen counter. I stop at her house to get my phone. Turning into her driveway, I see the neighbor's children across the street playing in the sprinkler. They are giggling and chasing the water as it waves back and forth. A white puppy is joining in the fun. Gospel music is flowing through the open windows. The sounds of 'Awesome' by Charles Jenkins fill the air.

My God is awesome, awesome, awesome, awesome
My God is awesome, awesome, awesome, awesome
My God is awesome, Savior of the whole world
Giver of salvation, by His stripes I am healed
My God is awesome, today I am forgiven
His grace is why I'm living, praise His holy name
My God is awesome, awesome, awesome, awesome
My God is awesome, awesome, awesome, awesome

He's mighty, He's mighty, He's mighty, He's mighty,
Awesome, Awesome

He's holy, He's Holy, He's Holy, He's Holy,
Awesome, Awesome

He's Great, He's Great, He's Great, He's Great,
Awesome, Awesome

He's mighty, He's mighty, He's mighty, He's mighty,
Awesome, Awesome

Deliverer, Deliverer, Deliverer, Deliverer,
Awesome, Awesome

He's Holy, He's Holy, He's Holy, He's Holy,
Awesome, Awesome

Provider, Provider, Provider, Provider
Awesome, Awesome

Protector, Protector, Protector, Protector
Awesome, Awesome

My God is awesome, He can move mountains

Keep me in the valley, hide me from the rain
My God is awesome, heals me when I'm broken
Strength where I've been weakened,
Praise his holy name.

> *Charles Jenkins*

I sit in one of the two oak rockers on the porch. Pots overflowing with red geraniums surround me. As I enjoy the scene, the children's mother comes to the door to check on them. She waves at me and retreats into the house. I'm lost in reverie until I remember I need to pick up Aunt Linn.

--

At the tennis center Aunt Linn is watching her doubles team play their weekly league match. The courts are in a well maintained tennis center surrounded by beautiful trees and flowers. The front entrance faces the river. Stadium seating guards the main courts. When I arrive she is surrounded by friends. Three of the courts have finished their matches with only the No. 2 seed playing.

Aunt Linn usually plays No. 2 so she's quite anxious. Each team has won a set and the score is 5-4, with the Smashers (Aunt Linn's team) in the lead. After a long round of volleying, Aunt Linn's usual partner, Jenine, serves an ace to win the game. Game. Set. Match. The Smashers jump to their feet and erupt into applause.

Jenine Brantley removes her soaked white baseball cap from her head as she leaves the court. Her white tennis dress is soaked, as well. After talking to the team captain, she makes her way to Aunt Linn, receiving congratulations and victory hugs as she goes. She chats with Aunt Linn as she exchanges her pink tennis shoes and wet socks for a pair of sandals.

Aunt Linn is an excellent tennis player. Her tall, lean frame lends itself to agility. At the net, nothing gets past her. Her ground strokes come fast and hard. She's also quite the fashion statement on the courts. The cute tennis dresses

with matching sneakers add to her winning spirit.
She's anxious to recover and get back in the game.

Chapter 11

After watching Aunt Linn's tennis team play yesterday, I'm hyped and ready for my morning run. I drive a few miles from town to the State Park. Arriving shortly after the park opens, I park next to the park ranger's truck. I recognize the driver as a childhood neighbor, Mark Harris. We make eye contact and smile. As we leave our vehicles, I notice he has maintained the athletic build our female neighbors admired. He said working as a park ranger gives him plenty of room to exercise. Clad in his beige ranger uniform, he looks the same as he did seven years ago. Mark removes his beige hat and embraces me. We chat briefly and he invites me to church which is Uncle Ron's church. He speaks very highly of Uncle Ron in reference to church and as a community leader.

As we say goodbye, I promise to attend church when in town on Sundays.

Grabbing my water bottle from the car, I start my run along a flat stretch. Thirty minutes later I've passed the lake, the camp site and ranger housing. Pausing, I drink some water then walk back.

--

Aunt Linn and I eat southwest omelets while watching the morning news. We talk until the coffee runs out and realize it's time to leave for the senior center picnic. Aunt Linn volunteers at the center and rarely gets to participate in activities during the day. She's determined to make the activity today.

Everyone is in place when we arrive. At the podium is the director of the senior center who I barely recognize. It's Aunt Linn's tennis partner, Jenine Brantley. She's wearing a navy blue, pin stripe pant suit. Her white, V-neck blouse is accented with a string of pearls and matching earrings. Her comfortable dark blue flats sparkle with a jeweled buckle.

After Ms. Brantley's brief comments, the picnic lunch is served.

She finally works her way back to us and says, "Hello. I'm glad you could make it."

"Hello," Aunt Linn and I responded.

"I enjoyed the tennis match yesterday," I said.

"I'm glad you did. I miss my partner. Make sure she follows doctor's orders. I need her on the tennis court to watch my back."

"Will do," I said.

Ms. Brantley continues to ease around the room as we finish lunch. She seems very at ease and attentive to the seniors.

After lunch, there is a craft session for the seniors. Aunt Linn encourages me to mingle and assist where needed. I sit with a gentleman who reminds me of my father. He is distinguished looking with a black shirt and gray tie. His shoes are shined and he has a huge smile on his face.

"Do you mind if I sit here?" I asked.

"Of course not, pretty lady," he said.

"I'm Paula."

"My name is Marvin Brennan."

"Pleased to meet you, Mr. Brennan."

"My pleasure, pretty lady."

"What are you making today Mr. Brennan?"

"I want to make a butterfly," he said.

"A butterfly?" I asked.

"A butterfly," he said. "You see, my wife – she's deceased – loved butterflies. She planted flowers that would attract them. She would sit on the porch and watch them for hours." Tears filled his eyes as he said, "When she died, I lost my best friend. So," he said. "I want a happy memory of my wife – a beautiful butterfly."

As we prepared the mold to make the butterfly, Mr. Brennan told me he is a retired pastor. He became a minister at 20 and a pastor at 35. He was a pastor when he married his wife, and in his words, "She completed my world."

"My wife and I had a wonderful ministry. We had four children who were active in church and remain so to this day. But, there was one thing that concerned me about my wife. She never said it, but I felt that she was lonely. I encouraged her to stay close to her friends and try to interact with other pastors' wives. I know that it can be tough on a pastor's wife at times, but she never complained. I loved her for that."

"I'm sure she loved you too, Mr. Brennan."

As we paint the butterfly, I tell Mr. Brennan about Jason's call to pastor. He gives me advice for Jason and tells me, "God has already told you what he wants you to do. Just keep doing it. It's not rocket science. When you're in unfamiliar territory, let God guide you. You're guaranteed a safe journey."

"You're right Mr. Brennan."

--

With Aunt Linn resting at home, I decide to visit relatives. I stop by to say hello to Shelley's mom, Nell. Nell is my mother's cousin. As I raise my hand to knock, the door swings open and there stands Shelley, wide-eyed and smiling. She's dressed comfortably in a red sundress. Studded red sandals adorn her tiny feet. We bear hug, scream and bear hug again. "G-i-r-r-r-l. I didn't expect to see you here," I said.

"I say the same thing," she said.

"You look wonderful."

"So do you," she said.

"What are you doing home?"

"I had a break from classes for 2 days, so I decided to drop in on Mom and take a breather. It's been a bit hectic at the university." Shelley is a college professor at the University of Tennessee – Knoxville.

Shelley also inherited my grandfather's features. Growing up, we were asked so often if we were sisters, we began answering "Yes." Actually, we did have that sisterly bond. We wore each other's clothes and were a fixture at each other's houses. My first boyfriend was a Shelley reject. She would never admit it. They were no longer dating and she was 'in love' with someone else. Shelley's reject was good looking and popular. I was young and dumb.

"How are things going with you?" she asked.

"All is well. Jason is good. Uncle Ron asked me to stay with Aunt Linn while he's out of town. It just happens to be a good time for me to take a break too."

While we move into the den I tell Shelley about Aunt Linn's injury. "How is she healing?" she asked.

"She's healing fine," I said. "The hardest thing is getting her to slow down."

"Aunt Linn is like my mom in that respect," she said.

"Where is Cousin Nell?

"She's running errands. That may take some time considering she left 15 minutes ago."

"That gives us some time to catch up. Do you have some news for me?" I asked.

"W-e-l-l-l-l. Since you asked." She thrusts her hand towards me and says, "I'm engaged to be married!" Once again we scream, bear hug and scream.

"I'm so happy for you!"

"Will you be a bridesmaid?"

"Of course, I will."

"My finance', Ashton, has a sister who is helping me plan the wedding. She'll be in town tomorrow. Join us for lunch."

"Sounds good," I said.

--

It's late afternoon. Aunt Linn is on the deck enjoying the warm weather and talking to Uncle Ron on the phone.

I thumb through some recipe books and decide to prepare chicken divan. It seems simple and we have all the ingredients. Fresh corn, broccoli, dinner rolls and tea complete the meal.

As I take the rolls from the oven, Aunt Linn enters the kitchen and says, "Smells wonderful."

"How is Uncle Ron?"

"He's good. Anxious to get home."

"I'm sure he misses you," I said.

"You think?" she said.

"I'm sure. I had an interesting conversation with Mr. Brennan at the Senior Center. He cherished his wife."

"Mr. Brennan was a devoted pastor and husband. His church did a lot of outreach programs for the city and his wife was a big part of their success."

"One piece of advice Mr. Brennan gave me as a pastor's wife was to do what God has already told me to do," I said.

"That's good advice" said Aunt Linn. "But, sometimes there is a need/project/job to be done that you may not want to do. You can do it, but you don't want to do it. There is no one else to do it. You do it until someone else can and will do it. Keep putting one foot in front of the other. Do what you can do until you can do what you want to do."

"That's good advice," I said.

Chapter 12

I think about Mr. Brennan at the senior center as I walk around the track at the elementary school. He's a wise man with a zest for life. Two other early risers are walking the track. One of the walkers is a friend, Melanie, from high school. Her damp, light blue blouse and white shorts indicate an early start around the track. Her dark blue baseball cap is wet, as well. After a cheerful greeting, I fall in step with her and we began catching-up.

Melanie married shortly after high school and now works as a supervisor for the Department of Family & Children Services in town. She's on vacation this week and has decided to start each day with some type of exercise.

"How is work Melanie?"

"Quite challenging! Too much work. Not enough employees. But, God is good."

"Are you still busy at church?" I asked.

"Oh yes! That's probably the one thing that keeps me sane."

"How is Nancy enjoying her role as pastor's wife?" I asked.

"She embraces it. Her biggest concern is her attire."

"You're joking," I say laughing.

"I'm not kidding," she said. "Don't get me wrong. She's an awesome First Lady. She works diligently at the church and definitely has her husband's back. When she became a First Lady she was worried about being under-dressed. A few years later, she was worried about being over-dressed. I told her to dress for Nancy. You're a Christian. You're going to dress to please God."

"Nancy is a beautiful lady," I said. "She's always attractively dressed. She chooses clothes that are flattering to her."

"Exactly," she said. "I told her everyone will not like the way you look, so please God and you'll be at peace."

We chat a few more minutes and say goodbye. When I leave I see a man in the window of the principal's office staring at me. There is something familiar about him. I get in my car and drive off. Glancing back, I notice the man is gone.

Chapter 13

Shaking the feeling that someone is watching me, I join Shelley and her finance's sister, Janice, for lunch at an Italian restaurant. We devour garlic rolls during animated discussion of bridesmaids, color of dresses and food for the reception. When the meal ends, we change the subject.

Janice is medium height with a dark complexion. Her short page haircut and bright eyes draw attention - - not to mention the short skirt she's wearing.

"Have you talked to my brother today?" Janice asked Shelley.

"He called this morning," she answered.

"How many times a day do you talk to him?" Janice asked.

"Don't start with me Janice."

"Paula! My brother is like a love crazed teenager." We all laughed. "He doesn't know which way is up since he met Shelley."

"She's exaggerating Paula."

"I'm not. He told my Dad he went to work last week with his shoes on the wrong feet." We laughed loud enough to draw attention to our table. After we wiped the tears from our eyes Janice said, "He was in a meeting with a client when he noticed his feet were hurting. He glanced down to slip his shoes off and could not believe it. His feet looked like Bozo the Clown." We howled in laughter.

We also laughed about dubbing Shelley's house the 'drop-off point'. It was my first date. Daddy said, "Yes, you can go." But, when it was time to go he told my older sister to go with me. I was embarrassed. Not to be outdone, we left home with my sister and took her to Shelley's house. Shelley was more than happy to be in on the plan. My father would be happy to know that my date was quite the gentleman. We took in a movie and went directly back home. Of course, my date was afraid of my father.

Janice was very personable and seemed to be genuinely interested in getting to know me. She asked about my work and Jason.

"So you're about to enter a new phase at church," Janice said.

"Yes, I am."

"Well, congratulations. I'm sure you'll make a wonderful First Lady," said Janice.

Before we left the restaurant, Janice told me her boss, Mrs. Carver, is a pastor's wife. Janice is a CPA at a large accounting firm in Atlanta, GA. She has become friends with Mrs. Carver and noticed that over the last few years Mrs. Carver has had several health issues. Janice believes Mrs. Carver may be internalizing her frustrations regarding issues at church.

"Did you have some advice for your friend?" I asked Janice.

"I did," she said. "I told her she's not the Pastor. She should leave the issues of the church to her husband. Her husband is well prepared for his role and he's surrounded by a staff of well qualified people to assist him. She loves to sing and is now focused on the music ministry. She seems to be happier."

"I think I'll take that advice," I said.

--

Picking up Aunt Linn's prescription at the pharmacy affords me a shopping venture.
Hall's Pharmacy has lovely porcelain figurines. I can't decide between two decorative eggs so I buy both.

It has turned dark when I leave the store. I notice a man near my car and that weird feeling returns. As I walk, I position the mace on my key chain. A few feet from my car the man speaks.

"Paula?"

"Yes."

"Paula Brown?"

"Yes."

"It's Larry Wiley."

Chapter 14

I want to throw a brick. "Have you been following me?"

"No. I've been doing some consulting at the elementary school this week. I've also seen you a few times around town. I just wanted to say hello."

"Hello, Larry."

"You look good, Paula."

"Thank you. I need to get home. Good night."

Standing a few feet from me is my former employer who embezzled company funds and used me as an accomplice. Wearing a brown tweed blazer, brown silk sweater and brown slacks he looks polished, as usual. His short statute and wavy black hair add youth to his fifty years. Of course, the company fired him. I, however, was never accused of any wrongdoing. Being oblivious to his unethical practices, as his office manager I basically followed his instructions. I don't know if he was ever prosecuted, but he did start his own company.

"Before you go Paula, I just want to apologize for involving you in any wrongdoing when you worked for me. I was selfish and greedy. I've worked very hard to turn my life around. I've made amends and paid the money back to the partners you and I worked with. I truly regret any embarrassment I caused you. Please forgive me?"

I look at him, astonished. "Forgive you?"

"Yes", he said.

"You used me," I said with irritation.

"I'm sorry."

"You humiliated me!"

"I know. Again, I'm sorry."

"You cost me my job!"

"Paula, you didn't have to quit."

"Excuse me," I said raising my voice. "How could I continue to work for a man who took advantage of a young, naïve and trusting woman?"

"I – I know. I know," he stuttered. "I was wrong."

"Yes, you were wrong," I shouted. "You were selfish, greedy and unethical. Go away, Larry."

"Okay, I'm leaving. But, I have changed and I hope that one day you will forgive me." He turned slowly and walked away.

"Not today," I thought.

After a few minutes, I calm down. I notice the hair on the back of my neck has relaxed.

--

The smells of a bakery travel through the house as turtle chocolate cookies cool on the counter.

The sounds of jazz saxophonist, Pamela Williams, fill the kitchen. My cellphone rings and I answer with a smile.

"Hey Babe," I said.

"How's my First Lady?" Jason asked.

"I'm good. I'll be better after a session with these chocolate cookies."

He laughed. We talked for thirty minutes -- as we have every day I've been away. I told him about my encounter with Larry. He asked if I forgave him. I said, "Yes, but he doesn't know it yet."

Aunt Linn wobbled into the kitchen as I was hanging up the phone.

"I love that man," I said.

"I hope you're talking about Jason."

"Who else?"

"Good. Now pass me a cookie."

"You know Aunt Linn, everyday has been sprinkled with good advice from you and other people - - advice that has eased my concerns about my role as a pastor's wife."

"That's how God works Paula. Sometimes the help we need comes from unlikely sources. We have to recognize it and be open to receive it."

--

Before climbing into bed, I bow my head, close my eyes and pray:

Thank you Lord for your inspiration this week. Thank you for my wonderful Uncle and Aunt and for using them to show me I am enough just as I am. Thank you for the realization that I can banish fear with courage. I now know when fear creeps in, courage will force it out. I love you, Lord. Amen.

Opening my eyes, I think of the song *'Thank you Lord'*. Softly I sing:

"Tragedies are commonplace. All kinds of diseases people are

slipping away. Economy down people not getting' 'nuf pay.

But, you've been my protection ev'ry step of the way;

I wanna say Thank you Lord for all You've done for me.

Folks without home living out in the streets, the drug habit

some say they just can't be beat. Muggers and robbers

no place seems to be safe. But, You've been my protection

ev'ry step of the way. I wanna say Thank you, Lord

for all You've done for me.

Oh, it could have been me, outdoors with no food and no clothes;

Or, just alone without a friend, or just another number

with a tragic end. But you didn't leave me to let none

*of these things be. Ev'ryday by Your power
You keep blessing me.
I wanna say Thank you, Lord for all You've
done for me.*

*Thank you for power.   Thank you for
protection every hour.*

*I wanna say Thank you, Lord, for all You've
done for me.*

Ending the song, I realize I'm no longer singing softly. Noticing also that my right arm is raised in praise, I lower it to retrieve a tissue and blot the tears trailing down my face.

Raising my right arm again, I say, "Thank You, Lord."

Chapter 15

Driving pass the high school, I hear music from the marching band as they practice on the football field. I execute a U-turn and drive back to the high school. Parking near a school bus, I assume the band is traveling today. Reminiscing, I think about the fun we had in the band while travelling with the football team. Before the football game, the bus was a party. After the football game, the bus was asleep.

The football stadium has a few upgrades. The concession area is new and the scoreboard is larger. I walk to the top of the bleachers, sit and watch the band practice. Reflecting on the week, as the band plays "Happy" by Pharrell Williams, brings a smile to my face.

The advice from Aunt Linn and the people I've met through her has helped calm my spirit. Aunt Linn told me that joining a minister's wives group helped her tremendously as a pastor's wife. She is a member of the Ministers' Wives Ministers' Widows Fellowship and applauds the work they do in the community. She also applauds the support the members give each other. Aunt Linn said, "There's freedom in knowing you're not alone with your challenges. This group gives us a confidential setting to freely express our concerns."

The marching band is playing a song I don't recognize when I leave. I think about Mr. Brennan at the senior center as I descend the steps. His wife may have enjoyed the Ministers' Wives Ministers' Widows Fellowship.

Chapter 16

Spending time at the high school stadium left me in the mood to pack for my return trip home. After talking to Jason, I began packing. Jason said he had a tough day at work. In his words, "I had to slay Goliath." He had developed a project, put people in place to carry it out and oversaw the initial work. When he left the site, the work stopped. He had to call in his reinforcement, Jesus, and Goliath is now dead. He said he will sleep well tonight.

I sleep soundly, as well - another dream:

I am a little girl running through a field of daisies, chasing a butterfly. After stumbling over a bump and regaining my balance, I notice I'm a few years older. Continuing to run, I encounter several more bumps and reach the end of the field. I've matured into an adult and I'm facing a wall. Looking back, I see the field of daisies was Goliath laying on his back. Each bump was a part of Goliath's body that I stumbled over. I matured at each bump.

The wall is Goliath's feet. How do I get over the wall? Goliath has on boots. His boots have laces. I climb the boots and hoist myself over the toes, landing at the bottom of steps to a building.

I wake up.

--

I walk up the steps to Mt. Aaron Baptist Church to grasp the extended hand of my husband. We walk into church together, Jason as the pastor, me with a clearer understanding of my role as a pastor's wife.

--

My mother often told me helping others ultimately helps you. I now believe that. Caring for Aunt Linn did as much or more for me than it did for her. I discovered what I feared was the unknown. What I forgot is we are challenged with the unknown every day. It presents itself in many, many different ways. The past week has shown me that God equips us for 'all' challenges.

I am fearless in Christ.

References

Good News Bible/Today's English Version:

PSALM 23:4
Even if I go through the deepest darkness, I will not be afraid, Lord, for you are with me.   Your shepherd's rod and staff protect me.

PSALM 27:1
The Lord is my light and my salvation; I will fear no one.   The Lord protects me from all danger; I will never be afraid.

PSALM 91:4, 5
He will cover you with his wings; you will be safe in his care; his faithfulness will protect and defend you.

You need not fear any dangers at night or sudden attacks during the day...

PROVERBS 29:25
It is dangerous to be concerned with what others think of you, but if you trust the Lord, you are safe.

ISAIAH 41:10

Do not be afraid – I am with you! I am your God – let nothing terrify you! I will make you strong and help you; I will protect you and save you.

ISAIAH 54:14

Justice and right will make you strong. You will be safe from oppression and terror.

LUKE 12:32

Do not be afraid, little flock, for your Father is pleased to give you the Kingdom.

II TIMOTHY 1:7

For the Spirit that God has given us does not make us timid; instead, his Spirit fills us with power, love, and self-control.

I PETER 3:14

But even if you should suffer for doing what is right, how happy you are! Do not be afraid of anyone, and do not worry.

Cathy Brown Hathaway received her B.A. from the University of Georgia and also studied at Georgia State University. She has received many awards for community work and resides in Chattanooga, TN with her husband, Gary.

Available for seminars, workshops and motivational speaking. Call (423) 987-7321.

Email: cathat44@gmail.com

www.ingramcontent.com/pod-product-compliance
Lightning Source LLC
Chambersburg PA
CBHW052003220626
47052CB00004B/1079